THIS BOOK BELONGS TO:

_____

THE CHILDREN AND GEORGE

DEDICATION

To my brothers and sisters, Ruby, Linda, Peggy, Dabby, Clarise, Roxie Ann, Evelyn, Undra, Tonya and Sonya, thank you. The memories we made in life and especially at The Branch are forever embedded in my heart.

WHO ARE WE?

WE ARE BUT A SMALL PORTION OF DIRT FROM
THE PLACE WHERE WE WERE BORN.
WE ARE THE FOOD AND THE DRINK OF
OUR MOTHER AND FATHER.
WE ARE THE PRODUCT OF THEIR
THOUGHTS, INHIBITIONS, AND SHORTCOMINGS.
OUR CREATIVE SEED, WHATEVER IT BECOMES IS
NURSED BY WHAT WE SEE, HEAR, TASTE, SMELL
AND TOUCH EARLY IN OUR LIVES.
WE ARE THE CHILDREN.

-CHARLES CRINER-

A MAP OF

Growing up in Athens, my sisters and I traveled from Mr. W.M.'s house to the Basher's and sometimes to the Lakeside Inn...this was our world. There was a stream that flowed just behind our house, "The Branch", as we called it. The Branch made our lives rich and rewarding; because, we frequently found new treasures.

ATHENS TEXAS

MR. FUNZY'S HOUSE

MISS NEIG'S

UNCLE ARTHUR'S HOUSE

THE BASHER'S HOUSE
(OUR BEST FRIEND'S HOUSE)

THE LAKESIDE INN

OUR WORLD

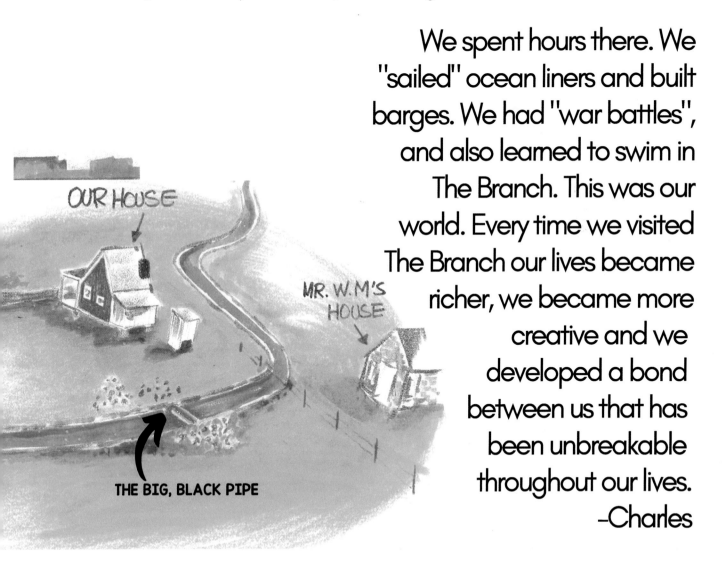

OUR HOUSE

MR. W.M'S HOUSE

THE BIG, BLACK PIPE

We spent hours there. We "sailed" ocean liners and built barges. We had "war battles", and also learned to swim in The Branch. This was our world. Every time we visited The Branch our lives became richer, we became more creative and we developed a bond between us that has been unbreakable throughout our lives.
–Charles

THE CHILDREN

Charles

Linda

Peggy

(Pinkey)

Ruby
(Cherry)

THE BRANCH

Once there were four children, Charles, Cherry, Linda, and Pinkey. They lived with their mother and grandmother in a small house, in the small town of Athens, Texas.

The children always had lots of fun when they were together; but nothing compared to the fun they had after it rained.

There was a big, black pipe that stretched across The Branch that flowed behind their house. When it rained in Athens, magical things happened at The Branch.

Sometimes when it rained, the water would flow over the banks of the branch. It flowed over the rocks that laced the banks and the flowers that grew along side of the branch. The water would also flow over the big, black pipe.

The children were very happy when it rained. They would huddle close to the window and watch the rain. They watched the water run past their house and flow into The Branch.

They knew that when the rain ended exciting things would be waiting for them at The Branch.

After the rain stopped and the sun came out...

the children would race to The Branch.

The children found wonderful things trapped against the pipe. They found fire wood for the stove and soda bottles to sale. The rain never failed them.

Once, they found a washboard their mother could use to wash their clothes. Each time it rained, it felt like Christmas to the children at The Branch.

One day the children found something different after the rain; something was trapped against the pipe.

That "something" was moving in the water.

It was alive, and it was splashing about. Pinkey imagined that it was a big, green monster with eyes like an alligator. Linda thought that maybe it was a shark, like the one she had seen at the aquarium.

Cherry and Charles both agreed that it was a catfish. They knew this because they had been fishing many times with their grandmother, and had caught catfish. They thought of how great it was for them to have found the fish, so they decided to keep it for a pet.

The children began preparing a home for their new "pet".
They stretched chicken wire across The Branch and
removed some trash that was surrounding the fish.
Charles stood behind the wire with his sisters and waited
for the fish, but nothing happened. The fish had been
freed, but it did not move.

The fish hadn't realized that everything had been moved from around it...ohhh, but when it did, with lightening speed, the fish dashed under the pipe and slammed against the fence. The fish splashed and splashed but it could not get past the fence and the children.

They did it! The children had finally trapped their pet fish. There was only one other thing they needed to do. They had to name it, but what would be a good name for a catfish? The children thought of many names but most of them were dog or cat names.

Finally, Pinkey said, "Let's name him George". What a funny name they thought, but they each agreed that "George" was a much better name than "Fido" or a cat name like "Missy". So, "George" it was!

Every evening after school, the children raced to The Branch to see their new pet, George. Sometimes George would hardly move but sometimes he would swim from side to side in the water.

One day Pinkey didn't go to school. Charles, Cherry, and Linda came home looking for their baby sister, but she was nowhere to be found. They decided to check by The Branch. When they arrived, there stood Pinkey with George, their new pet in her arms.

Charles took George from Pinkey's arms and placed him back into the water. He explained that a fish would not survive without water. Pinkey smiled and agreed with her older brother that George should be placed back into the branch so that it could live.

For weeks, the children would rush to the branch to watch George swim back and forth. Having George as a pet was very exciting and he provided the children with much joy. One day while the children were at school, the rain came. It rained so hard they had to jump over huge puddles to get home.

After the children made it home, they dropped off their books and headed to The Branch to check on George. Much to their surprise, their pet was gone. The heavy rain had knocked down the chicken-wire fence and pushed George miles and miles downstream. The children were very sad.

All of a sudden, Cherry turned and looked on the other side of the big, black pipe and screamed, "Hey y'all, look what the rain left for us!" There lodged against the pipe was a tire, perfect for Charles to roll, a doll for Cherry, an umbrella for Linda, and a little red wagon, just right for their little sister Pinkey!

"Christmas" had come again to the big, black pipe! The children were now all smiles.

As the children sat in the grass playing with their newfound gifts, their minds were still on George. They all agreed that the rain helped their pet George find his forever home, a place where he was truly free.

GEORGE'S JOURNEY HOME

George swam down the stream
past the big, black pipe,

past Mr. W.M.'s plum trees
    under the barbed wire fence...

until he reached the pond behind the Lake Side Inn. This was the perfect home for George! The pond was full of lily pads, turtles, rocks, and other fish that looked just like him.

George had found his forever home and he was very, very happy!

THE END

ABOUT THE AUTHOR

Charles Criner was born in the small East Texas town of Athens in 1945. He studied art and received his B.S. degree from Texas Southern University while under the guidance of the late Dr. John Biggers. Criner worked for NASA producing drawings for Apollo 11, as Advertising Director at the Houston Post and in advertising art at the Houston Chronicle.

Criner is most noted for his work with stone lithography, as well as his prints, paintings and drawings. His cartoon, the Johnny Jones series was created while serving in the Army and later adapted for the Houston Post's, The Job Crowd, The Dogs and a few others. Mr. Criner's art, ads, and cartoons have been featured in Ebony Magazine, Houston Business Journal, the Housing and Urban Development (HUD), museums and universities throughout the United States.

Mr. Criner resides in Houston, Texas and enjoys fishing and spending time with his grandchildren. He has three sons, ten brothers and sisters and many nieces and nephews.

To learn more about the author
please visit https://bit.ly/37otj7M.

14331265R00024